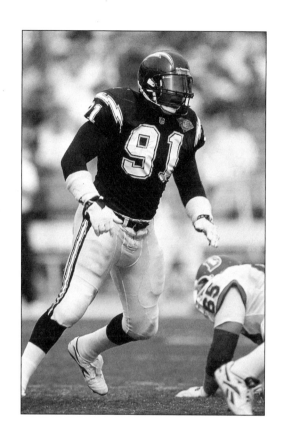

NFL ★ TODAY

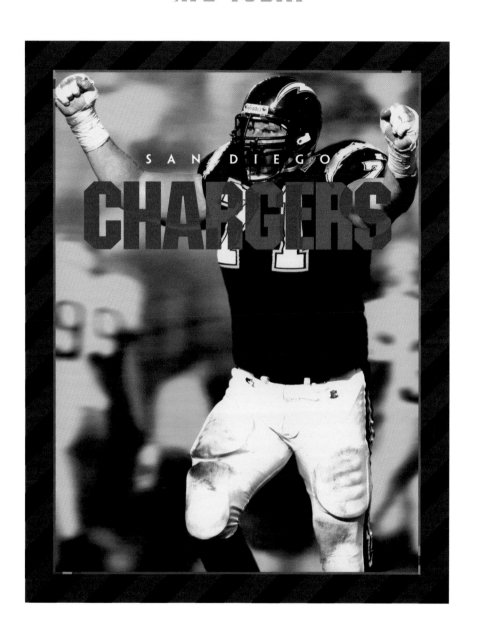

LOREN STANLEY

CREATIVE ✺ EDUCATION

Published by Creative Education
123 South Broad Street, Mankato, Minnesota 56001
Creative Education is an imprint of The Creative Company

Designed by Rita Marshall
Cover illustration by Rob Day

Photos by: Allsport Photography, Associated Press, Bettmann Archive,
David Madison, Duomo, Focus on Sports, Fotosport, FPG International,
and SportsChrome.

Library of Congress Cataloging-in-Publication Data

Stanley, Loren, 1951-
San Diego Chargers / by Loren Stanley.
p. cm. — (NFL Today)
Summary: Traces the history of the team from its beginnings through 1996.
ISBN 0-88682-811-2

1. San Diego Chargers (Football team)—History—Juvenile literature.
[1. San Diego Chargers (Football team) 2. Football—History.]
I. Title. II. Series.

GV956.S29S83   1996   96-15249
796.332'64'09794985—dc20

123456

For the most part, major cities in the United States are either growing very slowly or actually declining in population. One notable exception is San Diego, which has grown from a good-sized city into the sixth largest metropolis in the country. San Diego now has more than 1.1 million people. Forty years ago, the city had fewer than 350,000 residents.

Why is San Diego booming? The weather is one good reason. San Diego has perhaps the most sunny, yet mild, climate of any major city in the United States. But San Diego has also become a busy port city. It is also known for such attractions as the world famous San Diego Zoo.

The fifty yard line at Jack Murphy Stadium.

Paul Lowe was the Chargers' touchdown leader with ten TDs during the season.

Excitement and fun, that's San Diego. It's also a good description of the city's professional football team, the Chargers. For thirty years, the San Diego Chargers—the guys with the lightning bolts on their helmets—have entertained their fans with high-powered offenses highlighted by one of the league's most explosive passing attacks. Quarterbacks such as Jack Kemp, Tobin Rote, John Hadl, Dan Fouts and Stan Humphries have zapped the rest of the league by unleashing the lightning in their powerful arms.

The Chargers have also been known for coaches who love to use the pass. San Diego's first coach, Sid Gillman, had built a National Football League championship team with the Los Angeles Rams by relying on the pass. In 1959, Gillman and the Rams parted company after a couple of losing seasons. Despite that, several teams wanted to hire Gillman as coach. The team that did was the Los Angeles Chargers, a first-year team in the new American Football League. As a result, the experts made the Chargers the favorites to win the AFL title in 1960.

Gillman signed the team's first two offensive stars: halfback Paul Lowe and quarterback Jack Kemp. Behind Lowe and Kemp, the Chargers won the AFL Western Division with a 10-4 record. Unfortunately, the team lost to the Houston Oilers 24-16 in the league title game. It was to be the last game played by the Los Angeles Chargers.

However, the Chargers didn't exactly own the hearts of Los Angeles fans. The Rams were top dogs in Los Angeles, so owner Barron Hilton decided to move his team down the California coast to San Diego. Sid Gillman set out to make sure that the team's new city would have plenty of stars to cheer. Gillman managed to sign such great college players as running back

A high-powered offense and a crushing defense is a Charger tradition (page 7).

Keith Lincoln and defensive linemen Earl Faison and Ernie Ladd. These new standouts teamed with holdovers Kemp, Lowe and powerful offensive lineman Ron Mix to lead the first-year San Diego Chargers to the Western Division title in 1961 with a 12-2 record. But for the second straight year, the Chargers were defeated by Houston in the AFL championship game, this time 10-3.

1 · 9 · 6 · 3

Accuracy! Quarterback Tobin Rote completed nearly sixteen percent of his passes.

ALWORTH PROVES TO BE ALL-WORLD

Before the start of the 1962 season, the Chargers got Lance Alworth, a shifty wide receiver, in a trade. Alworth was a great athlete with speed, jumping ability, and the coordination of a gymnast. Alworth was injured during much of the 1962 season. So were a lot of San Diego's stars, including Lowe. In fact, no fewer than 23 players missed at least two games for the Chargers, who slumped to a 4-10 record. The following year, Lowe and Alworth were healthy again, and Gillman brought in a new quarterback, veteran Tobin Rote. Jack Kemp had been traded to Buffalo, and young John Hadl was having some trouble adjusting to pro football. So Gillman saw the need to have an old hand to steady the ship.

Rote wound up leading the AFL in passing in 1963 with 2,510 yards and 20 touchdowns, while Alworth caught at least one touchdown pass in each of nine straight games. "In every huddle," Gillman recalled, "Lance would insist to the quarterback, 'I've got the up! I've got the up!'" That meant Alworth believed he had learned how to break free from his defender on the "up" or "fly" pattern, which was meant to carry the length of the field.

Alworth's amazing play earned him a new nickname, "Bambi." The Chargers called Alworth that because of his running style, which resembled that of a deer. "Bambi, I used to love to watch him line up and take his stance," said Al LoCasale, "his free hand shaking, all the adrenaline pumping, all that energy ready to explode." Alworth wasn't the only Charger ready to explode. The offense averaged more than 28 points per game as the team moved into first place in the Western Division. Late in the season, Rote developed arm trouble, so Gillman handed the reins to Hadl. The young quarterback threw five touchdown passes in a 47-23 victory over Denver that clinched the division title.

Defensive end Ernie Ladd was a dominating presence at 6-foot-9, 295 pounds.

The Chargers were underdogs to the Boston Patriots in the AFL championship game that was played in Boston. If the Chargers feared the Patriots, they certainly didn't show it. San Diego tallied three touchdowns in the first quarter and wound up winning 51-10. Lincoln rushed for 206 yards, and Hadl and Rote combined for 285 passing yards.

HADL HANDLES THE PASSING ATTACK

The Chargers had won their first championship. Surprisingly, the team would not win another. San Diego captured Western Division titles in 1964 and 1965, but lost both years to the Buffalo Bills in the league championship game. The key player for the Chargers was John Hadl, who took over the starting quarterback position in 1964.

Hadl's trademark became the late-game drive to pull out a victory. "I call him Cliff-hanger Hadl," Gillman said. "If the game goes down to the final minute, John is the best guy in the league

A catch Lance Alworth would be proud of (pages 10-11).

Chargers quarter-back John Hadl aired out the ball for 3,365 yards and 24 touchdowns.

at pulling something out of the hat." In 1965, "Cliff-hanger" led the AFL in passing with 2,798 yards and 20 touchdowns, many of them to the speedy Alworth. Alworth had the best year of his remarkable career, as he accumulated 1,602 yards pass receiving, a team record that still stands.

Unfortunately for Hadl and Alworth, their heroics couldn't produce another division championship. Defensive stars Ernie Ladd and Earl Faison were no longer with the team. As a result, San Diego gave up more than 20 points per game in 1966. The Chargers slumped to third place in the division with a 7-6-1 record.

San Diego was no longer a dominant team. From 1967 through 1969, the high-scoring Chargers managed winning records every year. However, the team finished third behind the Oakland Raiders and Kansas City Chiefs, the two new powers in the

12

Western Division. Even though the team couldn't rise to the top, Alworth and Hadl stayed there. Alworth led the league in receiving yardage in both 1968 and 1969, and Hadl was among the leaders in passing yardage.

In 1970, the AFL and NFL merged. The Chargers were placed in the Western Division of the American Football Conference along with Oakland, Kansas City, and the Denver Broncos. While the Chiefs and Raiders were Super Bowl contenders, the Chargers were headed the other way. In 10 seasons in the AFL, San Diego had won one league title and five division championships. But the team had gotten old. And Gillman quit during the 1969 season.

1 9 7 0

Star receiver Lance Alworth snared 35 passes, averaging 17 yards per catch.

Gillman returned as coach in 1971, but he and new owner Eugene Klein didn't get along. After coaching ten games, Gillman decided he had had enough. Harland Svare, the team's general manager, took over the job. But Svare was replaced midway through the 1973 season by Tommy Prothro, a successful college coach at UCLA.

The team also had a new quarterback. In the 1973 college draft, the Chargers took Dan Fouts, who had starred at the University of Oregon. Fouts joined veteran Johnny Unitas, who had come in a trade from the Baltimore Colts. Hadl had been traded to the Los Angeles Rams. Fouts sat on the bench as first Unitas, and then James Harris, were given a chance to lead San Diego. The Chargers, meanwhile, finished last in the AFC Western Division in 1973, 1974 and 1975.

In 1976, Prothro decided it was time to make Fouts the permanent starter.

To provide Fouts with a talented passing target, Prothro used the Chargers' number one pick in 1978 to take Arizona State wide

1 9 6 7

New home! San Diego Stadium was dedicated before a crowd of 45,988 fans.

receiver John Jefferson. Prothro also brought in another receiver, Charlie Joiner, thanks to a trade with the Cincinnati Bengals. The team had the ingredients for a great offense, but Prothro wouldn't be around to see the final result. After the Chargers opened the 1978 season with a victory over the Seattle Seahawks, the team lost three in a row. Prothro resigned and Don Coryell became the new head coach. Coryell loved the pass, and he wasn't afraid to use it at any time.

FOUTS BECOMES THE PILOT OF "AIR CORYELL"

After a loss to the New England Patriots, the Chargers rebounded to defeat Denver 23-0. It was the game that turned San Diego's season around. "There's a different kind of feeling on this team now," said Fouts. "We feel like we're supposed to win every game. That's a big change when everyone expected us to lose." Led by Fouts, the team won 19 of its next 26 games during the 1978 and 1979 seasons.

"We're only doing what we do because of Dan," Coryell said. "He has such a flexible mind. He doesn't have all the qualities you'd want in an ideal quarterback. He's not a runner. He's a fine athlete, but he doesn't have the speed. But he is very, very intelligent, and he is extremely competitive and tough mentally."

In 1979, Fouts broke the NFL single-season passing yardage record when he threw for 4,082 yards. He also tossed 24 touchdown passes. Fouts combined with John Jefferson, Charlie Joiner, and the exceptional rookie tight end Kellen Winslow to lead the Chargers to a 12-4 record that year, good for an AFC Western Division title. Running back Chuck Muncie gave San Diego an effective ground game to complement a passing attack that everyone was calling "Air Coryell." Said Fouts, "We're going to throw

Chuck Muncie punished opposing defenses in the 1980s.

Tight end Kellen Winslow had a banner year with 89 catches for 1,290 yards.

the ball, and we don't care who knows it." However, the Houston Oilers managed to shut down Air Coryell in San Diego's first playoff game, 17-14.

The following season, Air Coryell started moving at supersonic speed. Fouts led the team to an 11-5 record, good for another division title. A first-round victory over Buffalo allowed the Chargers to host the AFC title game against the rival Oakland Raiders. A sellout crowd jammed San Diego's Jack Murphy Stadium. The Chargers took an early lead, but the Raiders roared back to claim a 34-27 victory.

Air Coryell was grounded, but only temporarily. The Chargers won the division title again in 1981, the team's third straight. Everybody knew about Fouts and the offense, but the San Diego defense was effective, too. Defensive linemen Louie Kelcher, Fred Dean and Gary "Big Hands" Johnson were dominant forces.

In the first round of the playoffs, though, the defense had a rough time. The Chargers jumped to a 24-0 first-quarter lead against the Miami Dolphins. But Miami took a 38-31 advantage in the fourth quarter. Then Fouts tossed a late touchdown pass to tie the game and send it into overtime. Finally, San Diego's Rolf Benirschke kicked the game-winner to give the Chargers a thrilling 41-38 victory. A week later, in frigid Cincinnati, San Diego lost its second consecutive AFL title game, 27-7 to the Bengals. "I can't tell you how much it hurts to come this far and lose two years in a row," said a dejected Don Coryell.

JOINER CATCHES ON IN HIS THIRTIES

The Chargers wouldn't have a chance to play in a third straight AFC title game in 1982. The team made the playoffs, but

Charlie Joiner finished his career with 750 receptions.   17

Wide receiver Wes Chandler made ten receptions for two touchdowns against Cincinnati.

lost to Miami in the second round. The next three seasons were hard on the Chargers. Defensive mainstays Dean, Kelcher and Johnson all left the club. Kellen Winslow suffered a horrible knee injury. Wide receiver Wes Chandler, who replaced the traded John Jefferson, was plagued by a series of ailments. So was Dan Fouts. Through all this adversity, there was one constant, one guy who was there no matter what—Charlie Joiner.

"I don't recall him ever missing a practice at all since I've been in San Diego," Coryell said. "One time, he cracked a rib and didn't take one day off. He said, 'I'll work through it.'" Said assistant coach Ernie Zampese of Joiner, "He honest to God believes that if you miss one practice, you'll lose something."

Joiner, small at 5-foot-11 and 185 pounds, had some speed, but his mind was his biggest asset on the field. Bill Walsh called Joiner "the most intelligent receiver the game has ever known,

the smartest, the most calculating. He could come off the field and tell me what had happened on the other side of the field. I don't know how he did it, a kind of extra sense, I guess."

Joiner became the Chargers' man to go to when the regular pass patterns broke down and Fouts was being pressured in the pocket. In one such case, Fouts said, "All I'm trying to do is look for a port in the storm. He [Joiner] is the port . . . . Having Charlie is like having a failsafe button. In our offense, it's up to me to decide who I'm going to go to, based on the coverages. When I'm back there in the pocket, I can tell when Charlie's going to be open, and at the last minute, I'll look to a spot and there he'll be. And he'll catch the ball."

Joiner's precise pass routes and his understanding of the coverages helped open up opportunities for San Diego's other receivers. After one game in 1984, a newspaper reporter asked Kellen Winslow why he was able to get open to catch ten passes that day. Winslow pointed toward Joiner's locker and said, "Ask him."

Most receivers see their productivity drop as they get older. Not Joiner. In 1984, he became the all-time leading pass receiver in NFL history, surpassing former Washington Redskins star Charley Taylor. When Joiner retired after the 1986 season, he had caught 750 passes for 12,146 yards, both NFL records. Those records have since been broken, but Joiner still ranks high on the all-time receiving and yardage lists.

Joiner's last season was also the Chargers' worst season since 1975. The Chargers finished 4-12 in 1986. The days of Air Coryell were over. New Coach Al Saunders had tried instead to build the team around a strong defense. In spite of the Chargers' failures in 1986, two young defensive linemen had great years for

1 9 8 4

Head coach Don Coryell inspired numerous imitators of his "Air Coryell" pass-oriented offense.

Quarterback Dan Fouts.

San Diego. Lee Williams registered 15 quarterback sacks, the second most in the AFC; Leslie O'Neal had 12.5 sacks, good for fifth place.

The improved defense and a healthy Dan Fouts keyed an 8-1 start in 1987. O'Neal was injured, but Williams, linebacker Billy Ray Smith and cornerback Gill Byrd led the stingy San Diego defense. Everybody wondered what had happened to the once-lowly Chargers. Who were these guys? The Chargers rose to the dizzying heights of first place in the AFC Western Division, but they fell just as quickly. San Diego lost its last six games and wound up third in the division. It was the beginning of the end for Saunders, who was fired after a 6-10 season in 1988.

San Diego hired Dan Henning as coach in 1989, but the team had another losing record. However, after the 1989 season, the Chargers found a man who would be the architect of San Diego's revival. His name was Bobby Beathard, and some experts called him the smartest man in football. As general manager with the Washington Redskins, Beathard rebuilt the team during the late 1970s and early 1980s, making Washington one of the best clubs in the NFL. Beathard became San Diego's new general manager, responsible for finding the players and coaches to fill the team's weaknesses.

Running back Ronnie Harmon was voted Most Valuable Player by his teammates.

A NEW WINNING ERA

In the 1990 NFL Draft, Beathard proved once again that he was a superb judge of football talent. He made linebacker Junior Seau, out of USC, the Chargers' number one pick that year. Seau went on to become the anchor of the San Diego defense—and one of the all-time great linebackers in league history.

24   *Left to right: Marion Butts, Billy Ray Smith, Leslie O'Neal, Kellen Winslow.*

Bill Belichick, head coach of the Cleveland Browns, offered this glowing praise: "Junior Seau is the best defensive player we've faced, I'd say, by a pretty good margin. He does it all. He can play at the point of attack, he chases down plays, he plays the run, he plays the pass. He's a guy nobody's really been able to stop."

Seau's achievements went beyond the playing field. He devoted himself to charitable causes in the San Diego area, including the establishment of the Junior Seau Foundation to combat child abuse and delinquency and to steer kids away from alcohol and drugs. For this work, Seau won the 1994 True Value/NFL Man of the Year award.

Powerful running back Marion Butts led the Chargers with 834 rushing yards.

Seau was inspired by his own childhood experiences to help others. As a boy, he overcame the challenges of a new culture when he moved with his family from American Samoa to Oceanside, California. Seau did not learn to speak English until age seven, yet he went on to make the California high school All-Academic football team with a 3.6 grade-point average. "When I was growing up," Seau explained, "my family didn't have a lot of money, but we did have a lot of love, and I had my dreams. The Junior Seau Foundation was created to help empower and educate young people so they can achieve their dreams. I hope young people see that dreams really do come true."

With Seau providing strength and character to the Chargers, the rebuilding effort of general manager Bobby Beathard had gotten off to a great start. But there were two more crucial pieces to the puzzle, and Beathard acquired them both in 1992. The first was a new head coach. Beathard's choice was Bobby Ross, who had led the Georgia Tech football team to a national college championship in 1990.

Natrone Means burst into NFL stardom in 1994 (pages 26-27).

Head coach Bobby Ross has made the Chargers consistent contenders in the AFC West.

"He's a tough, demanding coach, but at the same time, a fair guy," Beathard said of Ross. "He's not going to ask players to do anything he wouldn't do himself. People seem to respond to his coaching. He's going to win by getting absolutely the most out of his players."

The second key addition to the Chargers was new quarterback, Stan Humphries. Humphries had been a back-up in Washington while Beathard was general manager there. Beathard was now convinced that Humphries had gained enough experience to step in as an NFL starter in San Diego. And Humphries proved him right, winning the respect of his Chargers teammates for his leadership abilities and his physical toughness. On numerous occasions, Humphries played through injuries that might have kept other quarterbacks on the bench.

In 1992, Ross and his field general Humphries led San Diego to an 11-5 record, the AFC Western Division title, and its first playoff appearance in ten years. The Chargers upended the Kansas City Chiefs 17-0 in the opening round before falling to the Miami Dolphins.

But all that was a mere prelude to the remarkable 1994 season. San Diego again won the AFC Western Division—this time sparked by a new offensive star. Second-year running back Natrone Means set an all-time club record with 1,350 rushing yards. Meanwhile, veteran Humphries threw for 3,209 passing yards, giving the Chargers a balanced attack. In the playoffs, San Diego edged Miami 22-21 in the first round. Then, in a dramatic upset, the Chargers defeated the Pittsburgh Steelers 17-13 on the Steelers' home field to earn the AFC championship. Junior Seau sparked the defense by making 16 tackles during the game—an astonishing total for an individual player.

San Diego was on its way to its first-ever Super Bowl.

Quarterback Stan Humphries established himself as a leader in the 1990s.   29

Linebacker Junior Seau led the Chargers in the 1990s.

Mark Seay (#82) and Tony Martin (#81)—a dynamic receiving duo.

Unfortunately, the Chargers could not keep up with the San Francisco 49ers—who scored touchdowns on four of their first five possessions—and lost by a lopsided 49-26 margin.

But the Chargers were anything but discouraged. They returned to the playoffs again in 1995—and expect to keep doing so throughout the 1990s. The new winning tradition in San Diego has led to high expectations, including the prospect of a second—and victorious—Super Bowl appearance in the very near future.